Inn

The SEVEN DEADLY FINNS

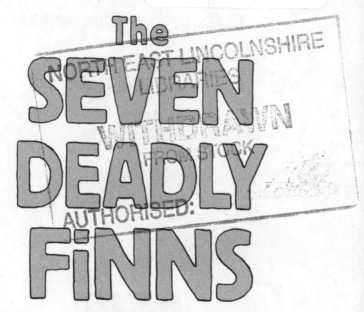

Books by the same author

*Granny Samurai,
the Monkey King and I*

*Granny Samurai
and the Brain of Ultimate Doomitude*

The
SEVEN
DEADLY
FiNNS

John Chambers

WALKER
BOOKS

First published 2015 by Walker Books Ltd
87 Vauxhall Walk, London SE11 5HJ

2 4 6 8 10 9 7 5 3 1

Text and illustrations © 2015 John Chambers

The right of John Chambers to be identified as author and illustrator of this work has been asserted by him in accordance with the Copyright, Designs and Patents Act 1988

This book has been typeset in StempelSchneidler and Block T

Printed and bound in Great Britain by Clays Ltd, St Ives plc

British Library Cataloguing in Publication Data:
a catalogue record for this book is available from the British Library

ISBN 978-1-4063-5008-1

www.walker.co.uk

**For my three
deadly daughters**

Mickey Finn

It was winter and Mickey was in trouble again.
It wasn't his fault, either. Really. It was the
snowman's.

"Except you made the snowman, Mickey,"
said Wowser his dog, though all Mickey heard
was, Woof woof woof.

Mickey Finn

But it was a brilliant snowman all the same: wide, fat, with five balls of snow piled onto each other and a hurling helmet on top with a traffic cone stuck to it like a giant luminous horn. It had taken Mickey all morning, and when it was finished he'd taken a photo on his phone so he could Wazzit it later.

"Bad idea," said Wowser, "that's like evidence against you." But all Mickey heard was, **Woof woof woof**.

"Say 'cheese'," said Mickey to the snowman. *Click!* **Woof**.

The snowman stood just outside Old Mister Noddy's front garden and was nearly two and a half metres tall. It was bigger even than Massive Feeney, Mickey's best friend Ogre's cousin's father, who had once played international rugby for Ireland and had his nose broken seventeen times. The helmet made it look even bigger.

The snowman was so big that it *loomed*. (Brilliant word.) To help with the looming, Mickey had poked two thick branches into its sides for arms and painted the ends of the branches to look like long, pointy fingernails.

"Or maybe fingernails that have been dipped in blood, like a vampire's," said Wowser, who still thought this was a seriously bad idea. Though as usual, all Mickey heard was, **Woof woof woof**.

"I know, Wowser," he grinned. "Old Mister Noddy is going to get the shock of his life. He'll get such a massive shock that his stupid red hat will fall off his head. He might even fly out of his socks."

Woof, said Wowser doubtfully – but about the socks. Mickey could easily be right about the hat.

The snowman was on the street side of Mister Noddy's gate. It loomed just beyond the lilac bush, half hidden by the twigs and branches, until you pushed through the front gate (if you were Old Mister Noddy) and suddenly saw it, towering over you. *Looming!*

Old Mister Noddy was ancient – at least forty – and bald. That was why he wore his sad red hat, winter and summer. Now it was winter and his nose was red too. And so was his temper. He was Mickey Finn's teacher. He taught screaming.

"FINN!" he would scream in class when he wasn't boring them with totally uninteresting facts. "ARE YOU NODDING OFF?"

"No, sir," said Mickey Finn, struggling to stay awake while his brain was being pulverized by history.

"ARE YOU THINKING OF NODDING OFF?" screamed Old Mister Noddy.

"Yessir, I mean nossir," stammered Mickey.

"Three bags full, sir," coughed Ogre O'Loughlin into his hand, trying his best to make Mickey laugh. And Mickey did laugh, which earned him an essay called: Why I Shouldn't Laugh in Class.

"Well, that's obvious," said Ogre afterwards, snorting. "Because class is unbelievably boring."

"Which was, like, unbelievably unhelpful," said Mickey. "Thanks!"

The laughing was partly – but not the whole – reason why he was in trouble now.

Mickey pressed SEND on his mobile and sent the snowman photo to Ogre. *Beep!* went his phone, and a text came back almost immediately.

Brllnt snwmn. Suprfrstng cool.

You bet, thought Mickey, and Wowser wagged his tail in agreement. The snowman *was* super-frosting cool, partly because Mickey had carefully poured two full watering cans of water over it after he had finished with the snow. The water had frozen into a hard shiny covering of icy armour, including the horn and the pointy branches. It gave the snowman an

eerie sheen and welded it to the sledge that
Mickey had built it on. He had borrowed the
sledge from his brother Lazy (who never used
it anyway) and had tied it to his teacher's gate
with two knotted elastic spiders. The elastic
spiders were for when Noddy opened the gate.
They were what made the whole thing work.

"Terrible idea!" shouted Wowser when he
realized what Mickey was up to. "Your worst
idea yet." But all Mickey heard was, Woof woof
woof.

Though even if he had understood what Wowser was saying, he would have ignored him. Mickey was an expert at ignoring good advice. He took a step back and looked at his creation. The preparations were over. It was time for the fun to start.

The fun was why Mickey was in trouble now.

Mickey picked up
some snow and packed
it into a hard round
ball. He smoothed
it off to increase
its aerodynamic
efficiency, then took
careful aim and threw it at
Old Mister Noddy's doorbell. *Ding dong*, the bell
would ring, and out would come Old Mister
Noddy, like a cuckoo from its clock, to see
who was there. When he didn't spy anyone,
he would come all the way to the gate to see if
anyone was there, either. Then he would open
the gate to look outside. The elastic spiders
would expand, and contract again.

Then the fun would start.

Mickey Finn

VUMP! The snowball hit the door and stuck tight. Right beside the doorbell. "Nice shot," said Wowser sarcastically. Woof woof, heard Mickey.

He made another snowball and tried again.

VUMP! CLACK! The second one whizzed straight through Old Mister Noddy's letter box. "Wow. Cool!" said

Mickey, and took off his gloves to text Ogre about what he had just done. Wowser sighed but didn't say anything.

Beep! Mickey sent the text. He put his gloves
back on and made another snowball. **VUMP!**
It struck the window just over the door. The
stupid doorbell was more difficult to hit than
he'd thought. *Beep!* A text came back from
Ogre.

Nce trow, wrote Ogre, and he wasn't just
taking texting shortcuts; Mickey's hamster
could spell better
than Ogre. **Tri
scatter efct nxt**,
read the rest of the
text.

Wow, thought
Mickey. *A scatter
effect.* Deadly!
Maybe a hamster

could spell better than Ogre, but Ogre had

better ideas than a hamster. **Good idea**, he

wrote back. *Beep!* More **woofs**.

Mickey started making lots of smaller

snowballs. A scatter effect was

when you launched them

simultaneously at the

target. The idea was

that one of them

was bound to hit.

It had to. It must!

It did. Here's how.

Mickey gathered up the snowballs, took

a step back, and threw them – all of them –

with all his might. And just as he did, the door

opened.

"Oh dog," said Wowser, and prepared to run.

Whoops, thought Mickey Finn, caught entirely empty-handed (now that he had thrown the snowballs).

Whiiiizzzz!! went the snowballs through the air. And struck.

"AARRGGHH!" shrieked Gráinne Feeney, age twelve, on her way to her violin lesson. Gráinne was the daughter of Massive Feeney, who had played international rugby for Ireland and had his nose broken seventeen times. She was already in a bad mood this morning because she found it was the quickest way to get what she wanted. And what Gráinne wanted, Gráinne got. She didn't want the snowballs, though.

Mickey Finn

VUMP! WHACK!

FLUMPF! POOOF! FLUB!

Five hard snowballs struck
her one after the other.
The sixth one hit
the doorbell. *Ding dong!*

Behind Gráinne,
Massive Feeney loomed.
"Who's at the door?" he
asked. Then he slipped on the

letterbox snowball, lying wetly in his hallway,
and crashed to the floor. "AARRGGH!" he
shouted, zeroing in on Mickey's
startled face down around the
lilac bushes. "I see you,
you little booger.
I see you!"

Mickey Finn

"He's seen us, Mickey," said Wowser.

"Let's get out of here!" And this time, Mickey understood. He turned and ran. Right into the arms of Old Mister Noddy.

"Here!" shouted Old Mister Noddy, dropping his shopping. "What's going on here?"

"Grab that maggot!" roared Massive Feeney, leaping up from the floor and jumping clean over Gráinne before pounding down the path towards the gate. A man who had played international rugby for Ireland and had his nose broken seventeen times wasn't going to let a simple snowball stop him. He reached his gate and yanked it open.

25

Mickey Finn

The elastic spiders stretched and tightened,
then pulled. The monster snowman shifted
suddenly, slid towards the gate and loomed
over Massive Feeney.

"AAAARRGGHHH!" he bellowed, and punched it right in the head. The head fell off and landed on Old Mister Noddy's shopping.

"My eggs!" shrieked Old Mister Noddy. "My eggs are crushed!" The headless snowman slid slowly past Massive, who shoved it away. Quick as a wink, Mickey Finn jumped on board.

"Hey!" shouted Massive.

"Come back here!" shouted Old Mister Noddy.

"Aaaargh!" shrieked Gráinne.

Woof woof woof! shouted Wowser, biting the elastic spiders in two and giving the sledge a good push with his paws. *What would Mickey do without me?* The sledge picked up speed and began to slide down the hill.

"Come on, Wowser!" shouted Mickey, but Wowser was already coming. He jumped up behind Mickey and they whizzed away together, clinging to the sledge and the remains of the monster snowman, while behind them in the distance Old Mister Noddy and Massive Feeney did a dance of rage until they slipped on the icy pavement and fell over together.

Mickey's phone beeped. It was Ogre. **Hey Mcky**, said the text. **STP IMMDIATLY!! Nddys hse izznt nr 6 its nr 7 OK. Srry.**

Srry yrself, thought Wowser, *and thanks for nothing.* But for once he didn't say anything, not even **woof woof**. The sledge was moving too fast and Mickey was too busy texting Ogre to see what Wowser saw: Massive Feeney charging down the hill behind them, and the

bottom of the hill coming up too fast before

them. Way too fast. Somebody would have to

work out a way to stop the sledge.

And quickly!

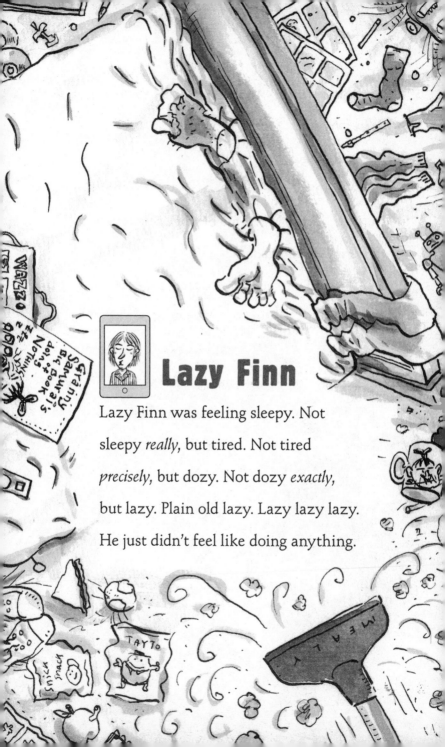

Lazy Finn

Lazy Finn was feeling sleepy. Not sleepy *really*, but tired. Not tired *precisely*, but dozy. Not dozy *exactly*, but lazy. Plain old lazy. Lazy lazy lazy. He just didn't feel like doing anything.

Lazy Finn

Not a thing.

Nothing.

Nothing at all.

No thing.

"Hey, Lazy," said his brother Mickey. "Can I borrow your sledge?"

Lazy considered the request.

"Come on, Lazy…" said Mickey. "You're not using it anyway."

Well, that's true, thought Lazy, lying in his bed.

"Thanks," said Mickey. He grabbed it and ran off.

Typical Mickey.

Probably up to something.

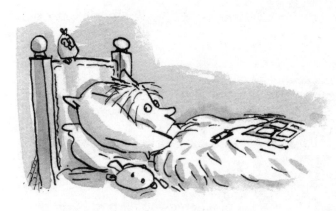

Like always. Unlike Lazy, who was never up to
anything. Not really.

The fact was, Lazy hadn't used his sledge
in so long that it was covered in dust and
cobwebs. It was the same with his roller skates
and his books and his tennis racquet and his
Wii – and his everything else, in fact. The sad
truth was that if he hadn't had a mother, Lazy
himself would probably be covered in dust and
cobwebs too.

 **Lazy Finn**

This is Lazy's mother, Ma Finn. She is hoovering her way into his room to get him up, even though it is already ten o'clock in the morning.

"Get up, Lazy!" she roared, and the hoover went, **Vrrroooooom!** "Gerrup ourra bed." Then she hoovered his toes to tickle him.

Fat chance. Lazy wasn't the slightest bit ticklish. Lazy was too lazy to be ticklish. Instead, he wriggled his toes and thought, *Well, that's easier than washing them.* Maybe his mother could hoover his hair as well. **Vrrooooooommm!**

Behind Ma Finn, Lazy's little sister, Dervla, ran past the bedroom door. She glanced in quickly but kept going, which probably meant she was up to something or other. Dervla had been up to something or other since she'd sprung out of bed at seven o'clock that morning.

Simply thinking about it made Lazy tired. First Mickey, then his mother, now Dervla. At least Big hadn't appeared. *Oh no,* thought Lazy. *Don't even think it.* But it was too late.

There was a pounding noise and his brother Big ran into the room and bounced on his bed.

"Gerrup, Lazy, you lump!" he shouted.

Lazy ignored him.

"Where's Mickey?" roared Big. "And where's my helmet?"

Lazy sighed. Where the helmet was, there was Mickey, and vice versa. Wasn't it obvious? There was a creak from the bed and Ma Finn swiped at Big with the hoover.

Wheeee!

"Get down ourra that," she shouted, "before you break it!"

Big grinned and did one more bounce. He bounced out of the window.

"BIG FINN!" roared his mother. "Come back here this instant and use the front door like anyone else!"

She was too late. Big was already clambering out of the bush below and heading for the garden wall. At top speed. Typical Big. He often left the house via the window, which was why the bush looked the way it did.

What a strenuous brother, thought Lazy, not even a bit insulted by the lump comment. After all, why bother being insulted by the truth? Then the duvet was snatched off him and his thoughts were drowned out by a high-pitched whine from his mother's hoover.

Oh, not again, thought Lazy. The nozzle had attached itself to Lazy's duvet and was trying to suck it up.

"Help!" yelped Ma Finn, even louder than the hoover. She grabbed the duvet as it disappeared into the tube and tried to yank it out again.

"Why don't you just switch it off?" suggested Lazy from his bed.

"Why don't *you*?" snapped his mother, and tugged just a little too hard on her end. There was a loud tearing sound and the hoover head burrowed through the cover and started sucking all the feathers out. **VROOOOMMPPFF!** Ma Finn cursed loudly. "Oh, fizz!" she yelled. "Lazy! Turn the hoover off!"

Lazy sighed and reached for the tennis ball he kept beside his bed for switching off the light. Now he prepared to throw it at the hoover button instead.

Lazy Finn

Nobody could say he wasn't making an effort.

"Oh, for heaven's sake," snapped his mother, still struggling with the hoover. "Why don't you just get up out of bed and *switch* it off? Hurry up!"

"Hang on," said Lazy, and threw. He was a better shot than his brother Mickey.

The ball bounced off the button and the hoover stopped groaning. With a giant grunt and a fine flurry of feathers, Ma Finn yanked her duvet back out of the nozzle. The ball bounced out the door and rolled towards the top of the stairs, where it disappeared from view, bumping gently from step to step.

"Time to change the hoover bag," said Lazy's mother opening up the hoover. "Look, it's full of feathers now. Go get me a new one."

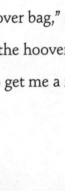

She gave Lazy "The Look".

He groaned inwardly. He knew what was coming next.

"GERRUP!" she shouted.

"GERRUP OURRA BED, LAZY FINN, AND CHANGE THE BAG. GO ON!" She gave him a hard poke with the hoover stick that promised many more to come if he didn't act IMMEDIATELY.

Lazy got up.

Lazy sighed.

This house is like a torture chamber of the Spanish Inquisition, he thought. He took the bag wearily from his mother and headed for the stairs. On the way he passed Dervla running towards her room with something hidden in her hands.

"Dervla," said his mother in a suspicious voice behind him. "Dervla!"

Lazy ignored them both. He reached the top of the stairs and climbed onto the banister. At least with a banister you could get downstairs without walking. Going back up was a pain, though.

He gripped the bag under his arm like a rugby ball and pushed off. He sped towards the hallway below at top speed. When he was grown up, he thought, he would buy a house with a lift in it just so he wouldn't have to climb back upstairs. **Whiiizzzzz**. He reached the end of the banister and slid off. His foot landed on his tennis ball, which had reached the hallway before him.

"Waaaaah!" shouted Lazy as his arms went up and he shot across the hall, crashing straight into Wowser's water bowl.

The water bowl flipped onto his head like a helmet, soaking him through.
The bag of feathers flew
from his grasp as if he had
flung it. Hard! It flew towards
Slasher, who was resting
on top of the coat pile near

the big mirror beside the front door. Slasher was Ma Finn's ancient one-eyed cat. He was covered in scars and so ferocious that even dogs were scared of him. He lay all day long on the coats and scarves of the Finn family, shedding hair and fleas and heaven knows what else, and nobody could budge him – not even Big.

43

Lazy Finn

Wowser refused to even try. At night, Slasher went out hunting and all the other cats and birds in the locality stayed well out of his way. He hadn't got his name for nothing.

Now he opened his one good eye and glared in astonishment at the hoover bag zipping towards him.

It hit with a mighty **THUMP!** and knocked him clean off his pile. But quick as a sword thrust, Slasher twisted in mid-air and clawed viciously on the way down. The hoover bag didn't have a chance. It burst with a loud

BANG! and feathers exploded into the hallway like a sudden snowstorm. They landed on Lazy and stuck. In two seconds he looked

like a giant bedraggled chicken. Slasher landed on all fours in front of him.

"Slasher!" shouted Lazy, too late. "Leave that bag alone!"

Slasher looked in alarm through his one good eye at the giant talking chicken before him. Sssssss! he hissed at the feathers floating around him. Then he turned and bolted through the cat flap. Things were just a little too weird for him right then.

Above and behind Lazy, Ma Finn approached the top of the stairs. "Lazy Finn!" she shouted. "What's taking so long with that bag? You'd better not be sitting around doing nothing."

Lazy sighed. What a strenuous beginning to an otherwise perfectly nice day.

Mister Finn

"Morning, bush," said Mister Finn as he strolled past the poor, stunted-looking specimen on his way to shovelling snow from the garden gate. But the bush didn't reply. How could it? It was just a bush.

Mister Finn

The bush was small and green, even in winter, with an empty bird's nest in the middle. The birds had long ago given up trying to lay their eggs and raise a family there. And who could blame them? Imagine how quickly you'd give up doing something if every time you sat down to it, Big Finn charged into your room and messed it all up again.

Mister Finn spat on his hands and sighed. The only thing worse than snow was shovelling it. Why wasn't Big out here helping, or even doing it for him, with all that energy? "He's worse than a tornado," he said. "He's worse than a hundred tornadoes. And I should know," he added wisely, holding up one finger. "Because I was once *in* a tornado."

"Really, Mister Finn?" said Ogre O'Loughlin, who had come over to play with Mickey and was now standing at the front gate, texting and watching Mister Finn scrape snow from the path. "That's amazing."

"How do you think I ended up in Ireland, Oliver?" replied Mister Finn, stopping work and leaning on his shovel. "It was a tornado that swept me here."

"What was it like?" asked Ogre, impressed. He had never been in a tornado himself and had sometimes wondered about it.

Text! text! text!

"Brilliant," said Mister Finn. "Like being on a rollercoaster and doing a parachute jump at the same time. And it went on for hours."

"Where did you live before Ireland?" asked Ogre, curiously. He had never heard this detail about the Finn family before.

"Tahiti," said Mister Finn, propping his shovel up against the wall and straightening his back. "Where there is no blinking snow. And pineapples grow on trees for anybody to pick."

"Pineapples?" said Ogre, doubly impressed. He liked pineapples, especially the tinned sort where you could drink the juice out of the can afterwards.

"Mickey never told me he was from Tahiti."

"It was before Mickey was born," said Mister Finn. "It was before Big was born, and he's the eldest." Then he brightened. "Did I ever tell you about the day Mickey was born?" he asked. Ogre shook his head. He had heard a lot of stories about Mickey, but this would be a new one.

"Well now," said Mister Finn. "I'd better bring you up to date. Grab hold of this shovel and give me a hand with the snow while I talk."

He handed his shovel to Ogre. There was only one, so Ogre wondered how exactly he would be giving Mister Finn a hand.

"We'll take turns," said Mister Finn generously. "You can go first."

Ogre started working.

"The Legend of Mickey Finn," began Mister
Finn, leaning back comfortably against the
garden wall, "started on the day that he was
born." He addressed Ogre. "Where do babies
come from?"

"Their mothers' wombs?" said Ogre.

"Normally, yes," replied Mister
Finn. "But not Mickey. Mickey
arrived on a firework."

"A firework?" asked
Ogre.

"A firework," said
Mister Finn. "I was alone in the
kitchen with my cup of tea, and suddenly
there was a loud explosion in
the sky followed by a shower
of bright lights. A firework."

"Wow," said Ogre, digging. Then he frowned. "How come Mickey never told me that?" he said.

Mister Finn shrugged. "Do you remember everything from when you were born?" he asked. Ogre shook his head. "Well, neither does Mickey," said Mister Finn. "Luckily he has me to remember it for him." He pointed to a patch of snow. "Don't forget that bit over there, Oliver," he said. "Now, where was I?"

Mister Finn

"You were in the kitchen," said Ogre, leaning forward on the shovel handle and pushing hard.

Snow looked light, but as soon as you got a lot of it together, it became pretty heavy pretty quickly.

"I was in the kitchen," said Mister Finn. "Indeed." Ogre's mobile beeped.

"Hang on, Mister Finn," he said, and looked at it. "That's Mickey," he said. "He's building a snowman," he added, and started texting back.

"He should have built it here," said Mister Finn, "and used up all this blinking snow. Then we wouldn't have to shovel it, would we." He shook his head in solidarity with Ogre. "Will I go on with the story?" he asked.

"Yes, please," said Ogre, sticking his phone back into his pocket and picking up the shovel again. "You were just saying about the kitchen."

"What kitchen?" said Mister Finn. "Ah, the kitchen. Right. Well, anyway, the firework went off and two seconds later there was a **THUMP!** in the garden outside. *What was that?* I said to the missus."

"Hang on," said Ogre, "I thought you were alone."

"If you keep interrupting my story, Oliver," said Mister Finn, "I'll never get to the end of it."

Ogre's phone beeped. "Sorry, Mister Finn," he said. "That's Mickey again. Wow, cool!"

"What's cool?" asked Mister Finn.

"Nothing," said Ogre quickly, then paused. "How do you spell *scatter*?"

"S-c-a-t-t-e-r," said Mister Finn. "Why?"

"Oh, just wondering," said Ogre. He texted quickly, then picked up the shovel again. "What happened next?" he asked.

"Well," said Mister Finn, "I looked at the missus, who had just arrived in via the door, and said, *What was that?* and

59

Mister Finn

she said, *Maybe it was Big playing football outside,*
and I said, *But sure Big has been in bed for hours
already,* and she said, *Well, I hope it's not thieves,*
and I said, *Well, I'd better take a look!* So I picked
up the sweeping brush just in case and got
ready to open the back door."

Ogre's mobile beeped again. He looked at it
and frowned. Mister Finn frowned too.

"Oliver," he said, "you'll never get the snow
finished if you keep on looking at your phone.
Plus it's not good for your eyesight." He pointed
to an icy bit on the pavement, just beside Ogre's
left foot. "There's a bit you
missed," he said. "Use
the edge of your shovel
to chip it away, like a
good man."

Ogre looked at him strangely and didn't chip.
"Er … Mister Finn?" he asked instead, suddenly
looking worried. "Does Massive – er, Mister –
Feeney live in number six or number seven?"

"Let me think," said Mister Finn,
and thought. "Six," he said.
"Massive Feeney lives at
number six. Old Mister Nod—
Nolan lives at number seven."
He winked at Ogre. "Why
do you ask?" he asked innocently.
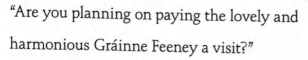
"Are you planning on paying the lovely and
harmonious Gráinne Feeney a visit?"

He stopped grinning as Ogre turned pale and
began texting urgently.

"I'm only joking, Oliver," he said. "Gráinne is
a lovely girl."

Mister Finn

That second there was a loud **BANG!** from inside the house. Mister Finn turned to look.

Some feathers were floating out through the letter box in his front door. Then, from further up the road, somebody shouted. Mister Finn turned towards the sound and frowned. There was a *thing* coming down the hill at top speed towards him and Oliver. It looked like a giant headless snowman with outstretched arms ending in large, pinchy-looking grippers.

"Uh-oh," said Ogre, switching his phone to RECORD.

Mister Finn

"Here, Oliver,"
said Mister Finn,
"we'd better
go back into
the garden.
Come on."

Mister Finn

He opened the gate. As he did, the cat flap flapped and Slasher came torpedoing out of the house in a flurry of fur and feathers.

"I don't like this," said Mister Finn, bracing himself for something – he knew not what. Yet!

"Me neither," said Ogre, leaping into the air to avoid the ever-dangerous Slasher, who was sizzling past him underneath. Ogre landed on the icy bit and slipped. "Whoops," he uttered, heart pounding and elbow cracking painfully on the pavement.

Then he realized it wasn't his heart pounding. It was footsteps, getting closer.

"Gangway!" shouted Big Finn, appearing around the corner and charging into their midst.

Big Finn

Big Finn was the eldest son of Mister and Ma Finn. He was not only the eldest, he was also the biggest and the loudest. He was like a hurricane stirred into a volcano stuffed into an earthquake.

BONG
BONG!
BONG!

HERE
T IS

Big Finn

"Big!" roared his mother as he pounded up the stairs. "The cups are cracking in me kitchen. Stop pounding."

"Big!" roared his father as he pounded down the stairs. "I'm trying to hammer in peace down here. Stop pounding!"

Mister Finn had a workshop under the stairs where he fixed things, most of them broken by Big. Now he was fixing his shovel. Big had snapped it while practising bashing a football long distance last week. Now he was practising bashing the stairs. At least that's what it sounded like from the workshop.

Big had large feet and the stairs were solid oak. Mister Finn felt like he was working inside a drum

while a giant beat on it from outside.

"Me ears!" he roared. "Stop running,
Big." Big stopped running.
He jumped instead.

Great, thought Slasher,
watching as Big soared through the
air towards him. *Brilliant.* Big landed.

BOOOM!

The pile of coats

under Slasher lifted ten

centimetres into the

air and the grandfather

clock shuddered, its

glass front swinging open.

"BIG!" screamed Mister Finn, sticking his
angry red head out of his workshop, a pot of
glue in one hand.

Big Finn

"BIG!" screamed Ma Finn, coming around the corner dragging a hoover behind her.

"Sorry Dad, sorry Mam," said Big, then stopped, and hit his forehead. "Fizz," he said, "I forgot my hurling helmet."

He galloped back down the hallway, jumped back over the hoover, squeezed past his mother once more and disappeared back up the stairs towards his bedroom. His squeezing turned the hoover on.

VROOOMMM!

It sucked the pot of glue out of Mister Finn's hand.

"My glue!" he roared.

"My hoover!" shouted Ma Finn.

"My head," groaned Slasher and closed
his one good eye tight.

Somewhere upstairs, Big
slammed a door and was gone.

"Right," said Mister Finn. "That's it.
I'm going out to shovel snow instead."

Mister Finn hated shovelling snow, but
at least it was nice and peaceful outside. He
grabbed his shovel and headed for the door.

Ma Finn yanked the hoover towards the stairs.
"And I'm going to wake Lazy," she announced.
"It's nearly ten o'clock in the morning."

And I'm going to move, thought Slasher,
opening his one good eye a slit. Of course,
he didn't really mean it. Instead, he scratched
himself, closed the eye again and went back to
sleep. *What an annoying family,* he thought.

In his room, Big Finn lifted up his bed by one of its legs and looked underneath. Where was his hurling helmet? There was a **CRACK!** and the leg broke.

"Fizz," he said, and put the bed back down quickly. More stuff for Dad to fix. He turned round and looked at the wardrobe. Maybe the helmet was in there? He grabbed the handle and the door came off in his fist. *Crisp,* he thought. *Why can't anybody make furniture that'll last any more?*

He reached in and pulled out an old hurling stick. Everything else came cascading down in

a massive avalanche. *Double fizz,* thought Big.
With all that stuff pressing against the door, no
wonder the hinges were so weak. He pawed
quickly through his stuff. No helmet.

Big frowned and ran his fingers through his hair. His head was as hard as a coconut and he didn't need a helmet really, but the rules were the rules. He wasn't allowed to play without one. Anyway, it would stop somebody else's hurley breaking on his skull. If only he could find the stupid thing. Why wasn't it where he had left it?

Something crunched under his foot. Big lifted his shoe and looked. It was a crisp, squashed to bits. He bent down and sniffed. Prawn cocktail flavour! There was only one person in the house who liked prawn cocktail, and that was his brother Mickey.

"Mickey!" he roared. "MICKEY!!!" Mickey Finn, his twerp of a little brother. That's who

had his helmet! Knowing Mickey, he had taken it for some peculiar reason all of his own. One that had nothing to do with the real reason for wearing a helmet, of course. Big turned and charged out of his bedroom.

Three seconds later he was banging on his brother Lazy's door – banging it open, that is.

"Gerrup, Lazy, you lump!" he shouted, leaping onto the bed.

Lazy didn't answer. How could he, with Big jumping up and down on his bed like a baboon.

"Where's Mickey?" roared Big. "And where's my helmet?"

75

Big Finn

Lazy sighed. Between Mickey and Big and his mother, it was impossible to catch any sleep in this house. It was starting to look like he'd have to move to Outer Mongolia or somewhere.

"Big!" shouted Ma Finn behind him. "Get down off the bed before you break it. Go on, get down!"

And Big got down. By jumping out the window.

"Tell Mickey I'm looking for him!" he shouted as he landed in the bush outside.

Tell him yourself, thought the bush.

"BIG!" screamed his mother at the window. "Come back here and use the door like everybody else. And don't you climb on the rabbit hutch! You'll break it. How many times do I have to tell you—"

But Big was already gone, scrambling over the garden wall at the back, one foot pounding onto the rabbit hutch for lift-off, the other knocking a brick from the wall as he went over.

Big Finn

He dropped into the lane behind on all fours.
Like Ronaldo, only better.

"Howya, Big," said Tiny Feeney, stepping out
of the way of the brick as
Big landed beside him.

"Howya, Tiny," said
Big, dusting himself off.
Tiny Feeney was
the son of Massive
Feeney, who had played
international rugby for
Ireland and had his nose
broken seventeen times. Tiny
was as small as his father was large,
and he and Big were best friends. They were
good together, too. Tiny was cautious where
Big was impatient; clever when Big seemed to

have left his brains at home; and faster than a greyhound over short distances. His real name was Seamusín but the only person who called him that was his horrible younger sister Gráinne, and then only to annoy him.

"Do you mind sitting still and doing absolutely nothing, Seamusín," she would say. "And I mean nothing! I'm practising the violin."

And Tiny would answer, "Oh, is that what the noise is? I thought the cat had got its tongue caught in a mousetrap."

While Gráinne looked around for something
to throw at him, he would exit. Which was
wise, as Gráinne had a good arm. If Gráinne
had aimed a snowball at a doorbell, for
example, she would have hit it. Every time.

"Tiny," said Big, "have you seen my brother?"

"Which one?"
said Tiny.

"The little
twerp one," said
Big. "Mickey."

"Yeah," said
Tiny, thinking.
"He passed me
on the way up
the hill this
morning."

"Was he wearing my helmet?" asked Big.

"No," said Tiny. "He was sitting on a sledge with Wowser pulling him along. Wowser was wearing your helmet."

"The little rat," snarled Big, pounding his hurling stick. "I'll teach him to steal my helmet."

"You think?" said Tiny, frowning. "I never heard of a dog stealing a helmet. A bone, maybe, or a dinner. But not a helmet. Are you sure it wasn't Mickey who stole it?"

"I meant Mickey," said Big. "He's up to some scheme and he didn't even ask me if he could borrow it."

"Because you would have said no," said Tiny, who was generally interested in what Mickey was up to. Because it was generally interesting.

"Anyway," said Big, ignoring Tiny's remark, "I have to get it back. Come on. We can follow them like trackers and catch up with them before they've gone too far."

"And when we find them?" asked Tiny.

"We'll scalp 'em," growled Big, and he pounded off at top speed up the lane, round the side of the house and out towards the road at the front. Tiny followed behind.

Weasel Finn

What a lot of stuff there is going on in the house this morning, thought Weasel Finn, peering through the mesh of his hutch at the bottom of the back garden. *What a lot of things the Finns are up to today.*

Weasel Finn

First, Mickey Finn had come out of the house being pulled on a sledge by his dog wearing a helmet.

Then Mister Finn had started banging something with a hammer, probably something that Big Finn had broken. Next, Ma Finn had begun screaming at Lazy Finn and hoovering to make him get up.

Why doesn't she just throw a bucket of water on him? thought Weasel. Cold water, too. That's what he would have done.

Then Ogre O'Loughlin had come over looking for Mickey

and found Mister Finn instead. Bad luck for him, as Mister Finn had hypnotized him into doing some work with one of his stories – *again!* And finally, Big had erupted through Lazy's window like a volcano, earthquaked his way through the back garden and nearly pulverized Weasel's hutch by jumping on it as he clambered over the back wall. "Howya, Tiny," Weasel heard him say, and then he was gone.

What a family, thought Weasel, then grinned. You could say what you want about the Finns, but at least they weren't boring. No, they certainly weren't.

Weasel Finn

Weasel Finn was a ferret. He was the oldest member of the Finn family, for two reasons. The first was that Weasel was nearly eleven, which would have only been as old as Mickey except that one human year equals seven ferret years, which made Weasel seventy-seven.

The second was that Weasel was actually Grandpa Finn, who had died in a ballooning accident over Africa eleven years ago and had been reincarnated as a ferret, which would now make him 147 years old, ferret and human years combined.

That's what Mister Finn said, anyhow, the day that he found him. He was squashed in behind a flower pot in the back garden, trying to get away from Slasher,

who was trying to reach him with his claws.

"He looks just like your father," Mister Finn said to Ma Finn after he rescued Weasel. "See!"

And Mister Finn held the skinny ferret up while Slasher hissed in outrage below. Indeed, he did look like her father, Ma Finn had to admit, with small furry ears and a fuzz of white whiskers around a long pointed nose. He even had eyes of different colours like her father did. The thought made her a bit uneasy.

And there was more.

"Look," said Mister Finn, holding up one of Weasel's paws. "He's missing one of his fingers, just like Grandpa."

Weasel Finn

Ma Finn gasped. "You're not keeping him in the house," she said firmly. "Even if he does look like my father."

But Grandpa had never lived in the house anyway, which was another strange detail. He had lived in a small shed at the bottom of the garden, where he had invented things, including the balloon that took him off to Africa. He only came up for his meals. He called his shed "The Hutch".

"All right," said Mister Finn, "we'll put him in the old rabbit cage beside the shed and he can live there instead. Grandpa would have liked that."

And they did. And he did. That was eleven years ago. Since then, Mickey had joined the family, and Wowser the dog, and Dervla, the little sister – called Whirling Dervla – and all kinds of assorted friends and visitors who were constantly coming to call and stay all day. The house was busier than a shopping centre. In fact, with all the rumpus going on there all the time, Weasel would probably have never gone inside, ever, were it not for his great weakness: biscuits!

Weasel Finn

Weasel loved biscuits. Oh, he didn't just love them, he adored them. 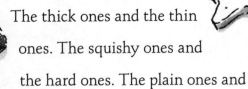 He worshipped them. All of them.

The thick ones and the thin ones. The squishy ones and the hard ones. The plain ones and the chocolate ones. The ones rolled up like tubes and the ones with cream in the middle. He even liked the ones with nuts on top. When it came to biscuits, Weasel had no favourites. They were all his favourites. The only problem was, he never got any, so he had to steal them. That was his big plan now.

He looked out through the mesh into the snowy garden. Big's footprints led from the squashed bush under Lazy's window all the way to Weasel's hutch. That was good. Weasel could use those. He lifted the latch on the hutch with a long tooth. Then he slipped through the door.

Outside, the ground was white and cold. But Weasel didn't care. The snow was the perfect camouflage. He took a deep breath and dived into it. *Ooof,* he thought, then started burrowing quickly towards the house, using the footprints as a guide.

Weasel Finn

If you were watching him from above, it would look like he was stitching his way across the garden, appearing and disappearing in the

snowy holes below.

Two minutes later his head popped up beside the bush.

"Howya, Weasel,"

said the bush in a squished voice.

"Howya, Bush," said Weasel, scrambling quickly up its branches to the window above, then slipping along the ledge to Mickey's bedroom window, where he peered cautiously in. The coast was ice-cube clear. He rubbed the window and looked again just to be sure.

Inside, Lazy was gone. Ma Finn was hoovering somewhere in the bowels of the house. A few feathers floated in the air. Weasel wondered for a second if Slasher had got his claws into some poor bird. What a horror that cat was.

He pushed his nose through the crack at the bottom of the sash and sniffed – once, twice. It paid to be careful when biscuits were at stake.

He sniffed again. *Yum yum yum,* he thought. *Come to me, my little nibbly darlings.* He pushed his head into the room after his nose and grinned. He was inside.

Then a hand seized him by the neck and squeezed. *Oh no,* thought Weasel, putting his legs into reverse gear, even though he knew it was already a million years too late.

"Wizzle," said a little girl's voice. "My little Wizzle."

The hand pulled hard. Weasel was dragged into the room, a line of hairs scraping off his back as his spine made painful contact with the window frame. The hand held him up. Dervla, Mickey Finn's little sister, grinned at him, showing all her pointy teeth – then planted a big wet kiss on Weasel's snout.

Aarggh, he thought. *No. Not now.*

"Wizzle wants to play with Dervla," said Dervla.

Squeak squeak squeak, said Weasel, meaning, *No! Absolutely not! Never!*

"Dervla wants to play with Wizzle," said Dervla. "Dervla wants to play Mama and baby." She jumped down from Mickey's bed and headed for her room.

"Help!" shouted Weasel. "Heeelp! Heeeeeeellpp!!" And in the corner of Mickey's room, Mickey's hamster Beowulf opened his eyes wide and stared out at the disappearing ferret.

"Hang tight, Weasel!" he shouted. "I'll send help. I promise." Squeak squeak squeak! But Dervla was already out the door and gone.

Weasel Finn

The air in the landing was full of sticky feathers. Dervla's ma stood at the top of the stairs shouting down at Lazy. Through the window looking out onto the back garden Dervla could see Big talking with Tiny Feeney in the lane. Dervla liked Tiny. He was fun to bite. She gripped Weasel tightly and tiptoed past her mother. She nearly made it, too.

"Dervla," said her mother in a suspicious voice. "What do you have in your hand?"

Dervla froze. Weasel wasn't ever allowed into the house because he made Ma Finn uneasy. Why, Dervla didn't know.

"Nothing," she said, turning to face her mother, opening one hand to show her. Her other hand squeezed Weasel hard behind her back.

"Show me your other hand," said Ma Finn, and Dervla swapped Weasel and showed her. "Now show me both hands," commanded her mother, who wasn't born yesterday, and Dervla stuffed Weasel into her nappy and showed her.

TIP   TOE

Aarrrghhh, said Weasel, but the elastic band of the nappy held him tight and muffled his voice. Shouting might have got him into more trouble, anyway.

"All right," said Ma Finn suspiciously, "just be good, OK?"

Dervla gave her a big toothy grin, turned and ran into her room.

Aarrgh

I really have to change that child's nappy, thought her mother, looking at the bulge as Dervla disappeared. Then a rattle from the front door distracted her and she turned away. It was Slasher, torpedoing through the cat flap below.

"Slasher," called Ma Finn, "is something wrong?" And she started down the stairs after him.

Nooo! thought Weasel, as behind Ma Finn the door to Dervla's bedroom closed and his doom loomed. *What a horrible word,* he thought unhappily, stuffed into Dervla's awful nappy and trying desperately not to sniff. He thought about Beowulf's "Hang tight, Weasel" and groaned out loud. Weasel Finn, explorer, inventor, biscuit-lover. Had it really come to this? His only hope now was a hamster, and that was a very small hope indeed. Hamsters were nice, but they weren't that smart. And

usually they were stuck in their cages or running around on their little wheels or something. In fact, the only thing

hamsters had going for them was that they were loyal like soldiers, and never forgot a good deed. And as it happened, over the years Weasel had slipped Beowulf a biscuit or two on the sly, and now it looked like Beowulf was going to try to pay him back.

Well, hang tight I will, thought Weasel bitterly as Dervla's hand of doom clamped once more around his neck and hauled him into the light. From one small furry animal to another. Hang tight indeed!

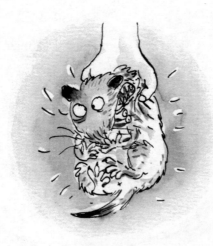

Dervla Finn

Dervla Finn was the youngest of the seven Finns but easily the most deadly. She was small and pointy, with a spatter of pale freckles on her nose like ice cream sprinkles, and red curly hair on top. Her eyes were mischievous and green like a fairy's. She had long, strong fingers.

Dervla Finn

"The deadliest Finn of them all," pronounced Mister Finn six months after Dervla emerged into the world. And he was right, too. That was nearly three years ago.

"Look at her crawl," her father would say proudly as Dervla raced up the stairs at top speed with Ma Finn chasing behind her with the hoover.

"Waaaaahhh!" yelled Dervla as her mother reached out and vroomed her by the nappy.

"Look at her bite," Mister Finn would marvel as Dervla wrestled a plastic bone from Wowser's mouth with only her gums. "What will she do when she gets her teeth?"

The answer turned out to be: chew until she
knew what every single thing in
the house tasted like.
Including her
brothers.

"Look at
her drink,"
Mister Finn
would beam as Dervla sucked her bottle
of milk empty in one deep gulp. It looked
like one of those magic bottles
where the milk disappears when
you turn it upside down.

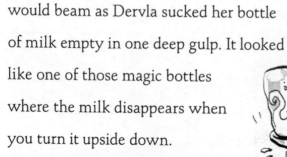

"Like the housekeeping money,"
said Ma Finn gloomily. "Look at my
shopping list. How much milk can that child
drink?" The answer was: gallons.

Dervla Finn

All of this happened when Dervla was just a baby. Now she was still a baby, but walking, and nothing was safe. Her father called her Whirling Dervla and loved her to bits. After Big and Lazy and Mickey, they needed some female balance in the house, he said.

And he got it. Because one Dervla equalled three boys any day, even boys as deadly as Mickey, Lazy and Big. And Mickey, Lazy and Big didn't argue with him. They loved their sister just as much as he did, even if she was a bit strenuous from time to time.

"When Dervla grows up, she's going to be a football team," said Big.

"Or a band," said Lazy.

"Or an army," said Mickey.

Or all three, thought Weasel, still jammed into Dervla's nappy and carefully weighing up his chances of making a dash for the window. He didn't care one bit that it was an upstairs window. The snow would break his fall, or possibly his leg, but even a broken leg would be preferable to the ghastly tortures Dervla had in store for him. Even another finger might not be too high a price to pay.

A sticky hand descended on his neck, cutting off his thoughts. *Ulp,* he ulped as Dervla hauled him into the open.

"Wizzle," she said. "Wizzle wizzly wooo." And she held up a small pink dress that she thought would go well with his fur.

No, thought Weasel. *Not the dress. Anything but the dress.*

Five minutes later, Weasel was wearing a tight pink dress and looking completely ridiculous. Dervla gripped him hard and

buttoned him up from behind.

"Pink Wizzle," she said,
and lifted him so he could see
himself in the mirror.

Weasel shut his eyes
tightly. And held them shut
as something soft came down
around his ears. *Not the bonnet,*
he thought. *Please, not the bonnet.*

But the bonnet it was. Dervla
tied the white lace bonnet under
Weasel's chin and burbled happily
as she knotted it. Twice!

"Wizzle babba," she said, then tickled Weasel to make him open up his eyes and see himself properly.

Being tickled by Dervla was like being tickled by a jackhammer, and Weasel's eyes snapped open like mousetraps.

Aarrgghhhh, he thought when he saw himself in the mirror, and he closed his eyes again. Now Dervla whirled him around and pinned him on his back to the carpet. *No,* thought Weasel. *Not the nappy. Please. Not the nappy.*

But the nappy it was. A "Wizzle babba" wasn't a proper Wizzle babba until he was wearing a nappy, according to Dervla. And Wizzle babba was what Dervla wanted to play.

She folded a hanky and laid it under poor Weasel's bottom. Then she shook about a kilo

of baby powder over him until he looked like
a cake in a baker's window.

Cough cough cough,
coughed Weasel,
trying to
wriggle out
from under
her fist.

But Dervla
held him with
her padlock grip, and
when she was finished

powdering she folded the hanky around him.
Then she sellotaped the whole thing in place
and pulled the dress back down. She lifted
Weasel up and cuddled him tight. This was to
burp him.

"Burpy burpy Wizzle," she said, squeezing him like a lemon. "Burpy burpy Wizzle!"

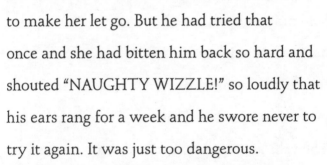

Aargh, thought Weasel, and for one wild moment he thought of biting her to make her let go. But he had tried that once and she had bitten him back so hard and shouted "NAUGHTY WIZZLE!" so loudly that his ears rang for a week and he swore never to try it again. It was just too dangerous.

A sound from outside made him twist around. Through the bedroom window he could see Mickey and Wowser zooming at top speed down the hill. A large man was chasing them. Weasel squinted, and recognized Massive Feeney, who had played international rugby for Ireland and had his nose broken seventeen times.

Hah, thought Weasel, *what is international rugby compared to being trapped by Dervla and made to wear a stupid pink dress?* Nothing, was the answer. He tried to picture Massive Feeney in a dress, but failed. Some things were just too hard to imagine. Then the window vanished from his sight as Dervla squeezed him hard again and flung him into a pram for his "sleepy time".

Dervla Finn

"Sleepy, Wizzle, sleepy," she said, smothering him with a thick fluffy blanket then tucking him in under a duvet and nearly boiling him alive with the heat.

She grabbed the handle of the pram and started rocking it, back and forth, back and forth, and singing in a voice that sounded like a seagull eating chalk, *"Rock-a-bye Wizzle on the tree top, when the wind blows the Wizzle will rock."*

Weasel winced. On the word *rock* Dervla shook the pram like Ma Finn trying to shake a blockage in her hoover, and sang even louder.

Urrrgghhh, thought Weasel. *I'm going to be sick.*

A loud **BANG!** from the bowels of the house distracted him. It was followed by a yowl that sounded like Slasher.

Weasel pricked up his ears, hoping it *was* Slasher. If somebody else was going to be tortured, it might as well be a mortal enemy. Dervla stopped her rocking and listened.

"Sssshh, Wizzle." She put a finger to her lips. Then she dragged the pram to the door and opened it a crack. Outside, her mother was standing at the top of the stairs about to descend.

"Lazy!" she was calling. "What's taking so long with the bag?"

A feather floated up through the air and over Ma Finn's head. She fluttered it away with her hand and it swirled towards a painting behind her on the wall, a ghastly portrait of some ancient cross-eyed relative.

The feather stuck right to his nose.

"Lazy!" called Ma Finn again. "I hope you're not teasing Slasher!" She started down the stairs.

Dervla pushed the door open further and waited for her mother to disappear from view. She had seen the feather too, and thought it might go well with Wizzle's bonnet.

"Fedder," she said, and nudged the pram quietly out of the bedroom door. "Sssshh," she warned Weasel, who glared up at her from the pram – though not so she'd notice, of course. That might provoke her.

Downstairs, Ma Finn started berating Lazy, who was lying on the hall floor.

"I'm not going back to sleep!" he yelled indignantly. "I fell."

Dervla Finn

"Where's my hoover bag?" shouted his
mother. "And what's all this mess?"

So many questions, thought Weasel in his
pram. *So much noise.* If it wasn't for the delicious
crumbly biscuits, he'd never ever ever ever *ever*
have come into this madhouse in the first place.
The pram stopped.

"Wizzle fedder," said Dervla, looking up at
the object of her desire.

Weasel looked too. The
feather was way up over his
head, stuck right to the nose
of the cross-eyed relation.

But it was too high for Dervla to reach.

Hah! thought Weasel, *serves you right—* Oo**ffff**! Dervla planted a big baby foot right on his stomach, pressing all the wind out of him. Holding tightly to the pram, she brought up the other foot. *No…!* thought  Weasel as Dervla grabbed his nose to steady her. She reached up for the feather.

Downstairs, Ma Finn opened the front door. "Slasher!" she called. Dervla let go of Weasel's nose then stood on it instead.

Umppf, thought Weasel, trying and failing to wriggle away. From his nose, Dervla now stepped onto the hood of the pram, gripping it with her toes like a monkey. With one sticky hand pressed against the wall, she reached up with the other and stretched and stretched. The feather was just one small centimetre away.

No, thought Weasel, seeing what was going to happen but unable to do anything about it.

Dervla flexed her toes and reached again. The feather was now only half a centimetre away. The pram trembled. Dervla's fingers brushed the feather. One foot slipped and she lost her balance.

One sticky hand pushed against the wall and the pram shot backwards over the top of the stairs like a barrel going over Niagara Falls. Weasel closed his eyes and gave up. Some things were just too big to worry about.

With a **RATTLE**, **CLATTER** and **THUMP!**
the pram thundered down the stairs towards
the open front door below. Ma Finn turned to
see Dervla coming right at her, riding the chaos
like a champion surfer and screaming with
delight.

Ma Finn

Ma Finn was tired. She loved her family to pieces but she was tired of them at the same time. She was tired of hoovering and cleaning up after everybody, tired of shopping and tired of cooking, tired of putting Dervla to bed at night and tired of getting Lazy up in the mornings, tired of wondering what Mickey was up to and tired of telling Big not to jump through the window onto the bush outside. She pulled the hoover into the hall and thought of something else she was tired of. She thought,

I'm tired of being tired. Once, when she was younger, she had visited Venice and had sat at a café drinking espressos and looking at the boats. Venice! City of coffee and canals. What on earth made her think of it now?

Mister Finn walked past, heading for his workroom. He had a pot of glue in his hand.

"Where's Mickey?" asked Ma Finn. "He was supposed to do the hoovering this morning, and I can't find him anywhere."

Mister Finn said, "I've no idea."

"And have you seen my mobile phone?" she asked. Mister Finn shook his head.

"Nope," he said. "I haven't." His wife looked at him suspiciously. Mister Finn didn't have a phone, which was fine for him, because everybody around him did and he was always borrowing theirs.

"Are you sure?" she said, wrestling the hoover past him in the narrow hallway.

"Yep," he said. "I'm sure. Cross my heart and hope to—"

127

BOOM!!

Big jumped down the stairs and landed beside them. Hard! Slasher stared with hostility as Big ran past shouting something about a hurling helmet.

One of Big's feet stamped on the hoover and switched it on. It snatched the pot of glue from Mister Finn's hand and swallowed it.

"Big!" shouted Ma Finn. "Get back here!" But Big was gone.

Slasher hissed and stretched out a claw to nick a hole in Big's favourite football jersey. It served him right for disturbing his sleep. Didn't everybody know that cats needed 23 hours of sleep per day? At least. He looked at Ma Finn and narrowed his eyes. *She's cranky today,* he thought. Well, they could be cranky together. Mrs Finn was the one human being that Slasher liked, and not just because she fed him. If she had been a cat – well, her and Slasher might even have got married or something.

Then a blast of cold air interrupted his thoughts. Mister Finn was now heading out to shovel snow and Ma Finn was yanking the hoover towards the stairs. *I would move,* thought Slasher, *if only Ma Finn would move with me.* He closed his eyes and dozed.

At the top of the stairs, Ma Finn paused and looked around. *Where on earth is Mickey?* she thought. *And why is it that everybody around here disappears the second there's work to do?* She opened Lazy's door. Except for Lazy. He was always just in bed, sleeping.

"Gerrup, Lazy!" she shouted, switching on the hoover. "Gerrup now." She poked him with the hoover and he groaned.

Look at him, she thought. If he didn't have a mother he'd just go on lying there, covered

in dust and cobwebs. She poked him again and the hoover snagged the duvet. Behind her, Dervla tiptoed silently past the door. The hoover began

to emit a high-pitched whine. Ma Finn shook it hard, but a pounding noise on the landing made her stop. "Big…" she began as her eldest son darted into the room past her. "BIG FINN!"

Big jumped onto the bed. "Lazy, you lump!" he shouted, bouncing up and down on his brother. "Where's Mickey? And where's my helmet?"

Lazy didn't answer. How could he, with the bed about to break like that.

"BIG!" roared Ma Finn, swiping at him with the hoover. "Get down off my good bed. Look at him, with his big dirty feet on my nice clean duvet. Big!" she shouted again, and Big leapt out the window, using the poor bush outside to break his fall.

"Tell Mickey I'm coming for him," he called over his shoulder.

Tell him yourself, thought Lazy.

"Come back here this instant and use the front door like everyone else!" screamed their mother. Then she thought, *No. Don't. Just stay outside. It's better that way.*

The hoover whined louder. The snagged duvet was worming its way into the hoover stick. In Venice, thought Ma Finn, wrestling with the duvet, she would be sitting sipping coffee and looking elegant. She yanked the bedcover back and forth. It was no good. The suction was too strong.

"Lazy!" she roared. "Turn the hoover off!"

Lazy let one arm drop out of bed and onto
a ball he kept there for switching on the light.
Exactly the kind of stupid idea her father would
have come up with, back then, before he drifted
away in his balloon.

"Hurry up!" she shouted,
and Lazy threw the ball.
The hoover stopped sucking and the ball
bounced out of the door and rolled towards
the stairs. Ma Finn wrenched the duvet free.
A flurry of fine feathers filled the air and she
sneezed loudly.

"The hoover bag's full," she said. "Go get me
a new one."

Lazy sighed theatrically. You'd think she
was inviting him to step into a torture chamber

the way he went on sometimes,
thought his mother.

"Go on, Lazy, and
hurry up." She prodded
him out the door then
followed behind,
trying to catch the
feathers swirling around her like
a cloud of bite-sized angels. Another bite-sized
angel, one called Dervla, peeped out of a nearby
room. Ma Finn didn't notice.

She stepped out onto the landing. That
painting of some cross-eyed uncle of her father's
stared down at her. Or maybe it didn't. It was
hard to tell exactly where he was looking. When
Ma Finn was small she had thought he was the
King of Ireland. But Ireland didn't have kings. If

Ma Finn became king, or queen for that matter, she wouldn't have to clean up after people, or hoover, or shop. How nice that would be.

Behind her a door opened and Dervla sidled out, her hands held suspiciously behind her back.

"Dervla," said Ma Finn sharply, "Dervla! What do you have in your hand?"

"Nothing," said Dervla, and showed her.

"Show me your other hand," said her mother, then, "both hands". After all, she wasn't born yesterday.

But Dervla passed the test. She wasn't born yesterday either. She turned and ran away.

Would you look at that nappy, thought Ma Finn. *It's like a balloon, ready to burst.* Then a Yowl! from downstairs distracted her.

Ma Finn

"Lazy," she called, "what are you doing? What's taking so long with that bag?" Slasher yowled again.

The poor cat, thought Ma. *What is going on down there?* She took a step towards the top of the stairs, then another.

"Lazy?" she called again. "What's going on?" If she was queen she would call her butler. "James," she would say, "go and see what Lazy is doing, like a good man!" And James would murmur, "Yes, ma'am." Butlers always murmured. A loud bang interrupted her thoughts.

"LAZY!" shouted Ma Finn, and started down the stairs. A small cloud of feathers wafted up towards her. Not again!

Somewhere beyond the cloud, Slasher jumped from the coats and shot like an arrow through the cat flap. A very large arrow.

"Slasher," called Ma Finn, and hurried down the stairs. At the bottom, lying on the floor again – wouldn't you know it – lay Lazy. Covered in glue and feathers. How on *earth* had he managed that?

"I…" said Lazy.

"…don't want to know," said his mother. She had finally had enough. She threw open the front door. "SlashySlashySlashy!" she called, and stopped. She looked.

Outside, something was just about to happen.

Something bad.

Ma Finn

There were Mickey and Wowser, clinging to what appeared to be a headless snowman, speeding towards the garden gate. There were Big and Tiny Feeney, charging straight at them from the other direction. There was Mister Finn struggling to open the gate before they hit him.

And there was Oliver O'Loughlin, Mickey's waster friend, filming everything on his phone. Oh, and there was Slasher, running into the eye of the storm, too late to slow down and change direction. The only Finn missing was Dervla. But wait…

And there was Dervla, standing upright on her doll's pram, screaming with delight and bumping down the stairs at top speed. One of her dolls seemed to be peering nervously over the pram rim; a very furry doll, it must be said. Ma Finn reacted. She tried to close the front door. She was one second too late.

"YAAAAHHHHH!" screamed Dervla, shooting past her.

Eeeeekkkkk! screamed the doll.

"Nobody move!" shouted Mister Finn (not one of his more intelligent pronouncements).

He had finally got the gate open, also a second too late.

"Mickey!" roared Big, his feet beginning to slide on the icy pavement. "You're dead!"

And Mickey, sticking his head up over the snowman and realizing he was about to crash, said, "Oh, crisp!"

"Told you," said Wowser, but all Mickey heard was, Woof woof woof.

With a sound like wet teabags being thrown against a wall, three junior members of the Finn family thumped into what was left of Mickey's amazing snowman: first Big, then Mickey, then Dervla. **THUMP, FLUMP, FLABPP!** They were closely followed by Tiny, Slasher and Wowser, who didn't even have time to woof.
FLLP, BLAP, SMACK!

"Deadly!" said Ogre, still filming.

The only Finn who didn't hit the snowman was Weasel. Instead, the pram hit it for him, flipping him out at top speed.

Eeeeekk! he screamed,
flying through the air in a
long arc, heading for the
middle of the road.

"Wizzle!" shouted Dervla.

"The baby!" roared Massive
Feeney, who was still running after
Mickey and had played international
rugby for Ireland seventeen times.

He launched himself into the air and
reached out for the poor pink child. He caught
her, too, like a rugby ball, and landed with a
grunt in the snow on the road.

"I have her, Pat!" he shouted to Mister Finn,
pleased with himself and his catch. After all
these years, by the hokey, he still had it in him.
"I have your baby, Fionnuala!" he called.

"What baby?" Ma Finn called back sharply from the doorway, where she stood surveying the damage.

"This baby," said Massive, puzzled, then looked at Weasel in his pink dress, nappy and bonnet. "AAARRGGHH!" he screamed, and threw the ferret away from him. "A rat! Getitoffme!"

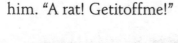

For the second time in two minutes Weasel flew through the air, only this time he didn't land. This time he got caught on something instead.

Something stringy. He grabbed it and held on.

"Is this the Finn family residence?" said a voice beneath him.

"It is," said Mister Finn. "How can we help you?"

Weasel twisted to look down. Just under his tail he saw a hand holding a bunch of strings.

"I have an order for forty red balloons for Mrs Fionnuala Finn," said the voice attached to the hand. Then it started to sing, *"Happy Birthday to you..."*

Weasel twisted back. Above his head he saw forty red balloons. Big ones, too, filled with helium. And he was caught in their strings. He grinned and showed his teeth.

"But it's not my birthday," said Mrs Finn, approaching the balloon man. He was wearing a hat that read: **BARRY'S BIRTHDAY BALLOONS**.

"Really?" he said. "Are you sure?"

"Of course I'm sure," she snapped. "I know when my birthday is, and it's not today."

"But we got a text," said Barry, "and ... *ow!*" he yelped, cut off in mid-sentence. "The balloon bit me!"

"It was the rat!" shouted Massive Feeney. "Look!"

They looked. Already lifting over their heads, Weasel Finn clung to the strings of the balloons and floated away.

A ferret didn't weigh a fraction of a Barry, and Weasel was rising swiftly now. A good nip of the gnashers was all it had taken, and Barry had let go of his balloons.

Enough with biscuits and the rabbit hutch and the horrible Wizzle torture: Weasel wanted to see the world. His moment had come and he was seizing it with all nine fingers. Who knew where the winds would take him, but he would find out soon enough. With a bit of luck, he might even make it to Africa.

"Don't say it," said Ma Finn to her husband as they stood and watched Weasel disappear into the pale grey yonder.

Ma Finn

The grey was because snow was starting to fall again. Around them their family stirred.

"You know," said Mister Finn after a moment, "maybe we need a holiday."

"Hurray!" shouted Mickey and Big – and especially Mickey, as it looked like his great snowman plan had been entirely forgotten in all the excitement.

"Hurray!" shouted Dervla and Lazy.

"Hurray!" shouted Wowser, thinking the same as Mickey, though all the Finns heard was, **Woof woof woof**.

"I mean," said Mister Finn to Mrs Finn, "*we* need a holiday. You and *I*," he added. "Together. Somewhere

warm. By ourselves. Without the children."

"Venice," said Ma Finn firmly, and smiled.

"Hurray!" shouted the children again, because they knew that meant they'd be going to stay with their granny, where they could watch TV and eat sweets and stay up late and get up even later.

"Deadly," said Mickey to Ogre. "You can come visit us."

"Deadly," said Ogre back. He knew Mickey's granny well. She wasn't a Finn, she was an O'Brien, but that was nearly as good. He showed Mickey one of the photos he had taken, and Mickey laughed. Then Big and Tiny laughed, and even Massive joined in.

"But what about me?" asked Barry suddenly. "Who's going to pay for my balloons?"

"Whoever ordered them," said Mister Finn. "And that wasn't me."

"But I got a text," said Barry plaintively.

"I don't have a mobile phone," said Mister Finn. "Sorry."

"And mine's lost," said Ma Finn, shrugging.

"And I don't live here," said Massive Feeney. "Maybe you should go after the rat instead."

Barry looked up into the sky. The balloons were now only a bright red dot, with a small pink dot hanging beneath them. What a stupid job he had. He must get another one immediately.

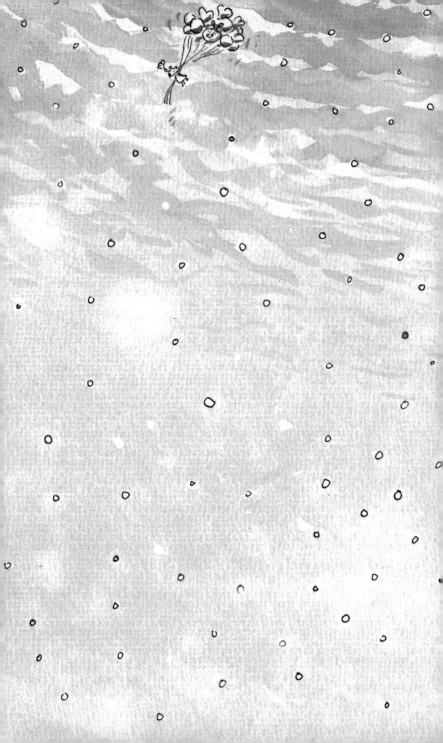

Beowulf

The Finn household was quiet. It had been quiet for three days now. Big, Lazy, Mickey, Dervla and Wowser were all at Granny O'Brien's, staying up late and eating sweets in front of the television. Mr and Mrs Finn were in Venice, sipping coffee and just sitting. Slasher was out prowling somewhere and hadn't shown up since the shock of the great snowman incident.

Epilogue

Maybe he will never show up, thought Beowulf, Mickey's hamster, as he snuffled around in the wood shavings at the bottom of his cage. That would be fine by Beowulf, who had never liked Slasher anyway. He snuffled some more and thought about Weasel. Weasel hadn't liked Slasher either, and he was dead right. Then he thought about Weasel floating off with the balloons like that. What a brilliant moment that had been!

Still, Beowulf would miss Weasel all the same, and he hoped that he'd come back again some time, even if just for a visit. That would be fun. They could sit and chat and eat biscuits together. Talk about the old days. He snuffled some more. His paw touched something hard under the wood shavings. That's what he

was after. He sat
back on his haunches
and scrabbled quickly.
Ma Finn's iPhone appeared.
He punched in the PIN and opened the
contacts list. What an amazing device it was.
He scrolled through the numbers: Ace Pet
Supplies, Barry's Birthday Balloons, Pizza
Express Yourself, Gourmet Guzzlers. He
stopped.

Gourmet Guzzlers. That sounded good.
He called up their menu and studied it.
Pumpernickel Five-Seed Bread with Chunky
Hazelnut Chutney. That sounded even better.
He began to text. The thing he loved about
the iPhone was the way the
words corrected themselves.

Epilogue

You didn't have to think about your spelling the whole time, which was just as well, as hamsters aren't very good at spelling.

Please leave food at front doorstep, he texted, **and ring bell before going away**. He pressed SEND with his right paw, then switched the phone off. Better to conserve the battery.

Then he covered the phone with the wood shavings and scurried over towards his wheel. It was bright orange and attached to the side of the cage. A couple of rounds before dinner was just the thing, he thought, to work up a nice appetite. He stepped into the wheel and started running.

John Chambers

was born in the West of Ireland and
grew up in Dublin. He writes and draws
for a living. When he was at school
he used to make up stories about his
teachers, for which he sometimes
got in trouble. If he had
known it was going to turn into
his job, he mightn't have bothered
going to school in the first place.
John has three daughters
and lives in a big city. If you want
to see more stuff about the Finns, go to
www.thesevendeadlyfinns.com
Hopefully, John will have got around
to doing some by then.